Lena's Day

WRITTEN BY
Emily Jackson

ILLUSTRATED BY
Charlene Chua

Lena was fast asleep when she heard her younger brother's voice.

"It's time to get up, Lena!" Tulugak exclaimed. He ran off to the kitchen to get his breakfast.

Lena dragged herself out of bed and walked into the kitchen. She saw her *amaamak* making toast. Tulugak was already eating scrambled eggs.

"*Ublaakkut, panik*! What would you like for breakfast?" asked her amaamak.

Lena looked around the kitchen at all the different things she could eat. She saw bread, tea, and even cookies!

"Cereal, please," Lena said. "And do we have any apples?"

After Lena and Tulugak ate breakfast, they got dressed, brushed their teeth, and put on their outdoor clothes. The cold October breeze made Lena feel more awake.

As they crunched along the frosty ground, Lena noticed that her toes felt a little cold. Wiggling her left foot, she saw her duffle sock peeking through the toe of her *kamik*. Her *anaanattiaq* had made her *kammak*, and they were her favourite things to wear. Lena showed her brother the hole.

"Tell Amaamak and *Aappak* so you can get new kammak!" Tulugak suggested.

Lena frowned. She didn't want new kammak. She wanted these ones.

Lena was excited to get to school. After hanging up her outdoor clothing, she headed to the gym to play some games with her friends. When the bell rang for morning announcements, Lena sat down and listened.

"After school, there will be dodgeball and hockey at the community centre for students in Grades 1, 2, and 3. Remember to bring your shoes!" Lena's principal said.

Lena couldn't wait for dodgeball!

The first subject of the day was language arts. Lena enjoyed writing, but she was in the silent reading group first. She peeked over the top of her book at her classmates working. It was very quiet, and she felt restless. She thought for a minute and came up with a hilarious idea!

Lena got up from her cushion and snuck under a table. She started reading out loud in a silly voice. A few kids giggled. Her friend Mary frowned at her and erased some of her writing. Hayok, who was trying to read with their teacher, stumbled and had to start again.

9

"Lena, come out from under there," Lena heard her teacher say. She did not sound happy.

Lena crawled out from under the table and stood up.

"That was very disrespectful," Lena's teacher continued. "Your classmates are trying to concentrate, and you interrupted them."

"I'm sorry," Lena said, looking down at the floor.

"You should be apologizing to your friends."

Lena looked around the classroom. "Sorry, everyone," she said. Mary and Hayok smiled at her.

11

Finally, it was time for gym class. As her teacher explained what they would be doing, Lena's class couldn't hide their excitement. They were going to be doing Inuit games!

"*Alianaaq!*" they cheered.

Lena won at leg wrestling and the muskox fight. They ended the class with Lena's favourite game: one-foot high kick. Lena kicked as high as she could, but Hayok kicked higher. Everyone clapped and a few people gave Hayok a high five. Lena wished she had won, and she started to walk away without saying anything. But seeing Hayok so happy made her happy. She decided to give her a high five, too.

After gym class, Lena was very hungry. She was glad it was lunchtime. She put her kammak on and sighed. The hole was getting bigger. She wondered how she could hide the hole from her parents.

"Hey, Lena, do you want to play outside with us during lunch?" asked her friend Mary.

Lena loved to play outside, but she knew her anaanattiaq was expecting her. The bell rang for lunch.

"Thanks, maybe another time!" Lena called to her friends as she found Tulugak. Together, they raced to their anaanattiaq's house.

Lena's stomach growled when she opened the door. She quickly pulled off her kammak and hid them under the pile of shoes in the porch. She hoped her anaanattiaq wouldn't see the hole.

Fish soup was steaming on the stove, and her anaanattiaq was pulling a sizzling piece of bannock from the pan. They talked about their mornings as they ate lunch. Lena felt warm and happy, and she was glad she had decided not to stay and play with her friends at lunch.

When Lena got back to school, Lena's teacher reminded the class that they would be spending the afternoon drum dancing with Haogak, an Elder, and Dan, an expert drum dancer.

As Haogak and Dan explained where drum dancing came from and how to do it, Lena and Hayok whispered excitedly. They couldn't wait to try! But soon, Lena noticed that Haogak and Dan had stopped talking and were looking right at her.

Dan said, "I can tell you two are excited to try. But how will you know how to dance and why you are doing it if you don't stop talking? Respect what Haogak is saying by listening closely and you will learn much faster."

Lena felt embarrassed and sad. But Haogak smiled at her and began speaking again. Lena smiled back and listened carefully to everything she had to say.

The bell rang at 3:45. School was over, and it was time for dodgeball! Lena and her friends ran to the community centre as fast as they could. As she moved around the gym, dodging and throwing, Lena saw that some other kids were playing hockey. *That would be fun, too*, Lena thought. *But I've already decided to play dodgeball, and I shouldn't let my team down. If those kids are playing hockey again tomorrow, I can join them then.*

After dodgeball, Lena walked home with Mary. The girls were tired but happy. So many great things had happened today! As they walked home, they decided to get a little snack from the store. They each had some money in their jackets, and together they were able to buy a small bag of chips, two suckers, and some gum.

The girls gobbled up their treats. Suddenly, Lena remembered something.

"Oh no," Lena said. "I forgot I was trying to save money for a new hockey jersey!"

As Lena waved goodbye to Mary, she noticed her stomach started to hurt a bit. She hoped the ache would go away before dinner.

Lena walked up the steps to her house, closed the door, and pulled off her kammak. She looked carefully at the hole. She did not want to get new kammak, but her foot was cold and it was only October. She nervously tucked them under the bench as her amaamak called her from the kitchen.

"Hi, Lena! Dinner is almost ready!"

Lena and her family sat down to dinner. Everyone had a juicy homemade *tuktu* burger with carrots and dip. Lena piled her burger high with tomatoes and ketchup. She was glad her amaamak had made country food tonight. Her stomach finally started to feel better.

After dinner, Lena wanted to join her aappak to watch some hockey. But she knew she had to do her homework assignment first.

Grabbing the folded sheet of paper from her jacket pocket, she pulled out a chair at the kitchen table. She worked quietly on her homework. When she got stuck, she asked her amaamak for help.

The game was still on when she finished her homework, so she watched the last few minutes with her aappak.

After the game, Lena said goodnight and got ready for bed.

Once she had brushed her teeth and gotten into bed, Lena's amaamak came in to read with her. They read together most nights before bed, and they were halfway through a new novel. It was really interesting, and Lena liked all the different voices her amaamak did for the characters.

When Lena's amaamak finished the chapter, she started to say goodnight. Lena thought for a minute, and then she spoke.

"Amaamak? My kamik has a hole in it. I'm sorry, I don't know how it happened. I don't want new kammak, but my foot is getting cold. What do you think I should do?" Lena spoke quickly. She was nervous about what her amaamak might say.

Lena's amaamak smiled. "Lena, that is nothing to worry about. Anaanattiaq can fix anything. She repaired my kammak many times when I was a kid! Let's go to her house tomorrow and show her."

Lena smiled wide and sighed in relief. She was glad she decided to ask her amaamak for advice.

Lena's amaamak said goodnight and shut the door. Lena snuggled in tighter and closed her eyes. *What a busy day,* she thought. *I wonder what will happen tomorrow!*

Inuinnaqtun Glossary

Notes on Inuinnaqtun pronunciation: There are some sounds in Inuinnaqtun that may be unfamiliar to English speakers. The pronunciations below convey those sounds in the following ways:

- A double vowel (for example, *aa, ee*) creates a long vowel sound.
- Capitalized letters indicate the emphasis.
- **q** is a "uvular" sound, which is a sound that comes from the very back of the throat (the uvula). This is different from the **k** sound, which is the same as the typical English **k** sound.

aappak AAP-pak	father
Alianaaq a-li-a-NAAQ	an expression of joy
amaamak a-MAA-mak	mother

anaanattiaq a-NAA-nat-ti-aq	grandmother
Haogak HOW-gak	name
Hayok HA-yok	name
kamik ka-MIK	one skin boot
kammak KAM-mak	two skin boots
panik PA-nik	daughter
tuktu TOOK-tu	caribou
Tulugak TU-lu-gak	name, meaning "raven"
ublaakkut ub-LAAK-kut	good morning

For more Inuinnaqtun and Inuktitut pronunciation resources, please visit inhabiteducation.com/inuitnipingit.

Nunavummi